Pip and Posy

www.worldofpipandposy.com

First published 2011 by Nosy Crow Ltd
The Crow's Nest, 14 Baden Place
Crosby Row, London SE1 1YW
www.nosycrow.com

This edition first published 2013

ISBN 978 0 85763 078 0

A CIP catalogue record for this book is available from the British Library.

Printed in China

Papers used by Nosy Crow are made from wood grown in sustainable forests.

9 8

Pip and Posy

The Little Puddle

Axel Scheffler

Pip came to play at Posy's house.

He hung up his coat and
took off his wellies.

"What shall we play?"
said Posy.

First, they decided to take
their babies for a walk.

Next, they built a big train track and a town.

Then they stopped for a snack.

Pip was **very** thirsty!

After that, Pip and Posy
pretended to be lions.

And they had such fun **roaring** that Pip forgot he needed a wee.

Suddenly, there was
a little puddle
on the floor.

Oh dear!

"Never mind, Pip,"
said Posy.

“Everyone has accidents
sometimes.”

Posy gave Pip some of her clothes to wear.

They spent the rest of the day
painting pictures.

And the next time Pip had to have a wee,
he did it in the potty.

All by himself.

Then it was time for a bath.
With lots of bubbles.

Hooray!